P9-EJT-466

CALGARY PUBLIC LIBRARY
NOVEMBER 2015

The Knightly Campout

adapted by Cordelia Evans
based on the screenplay written by Simon Nicholson

Ready-to-Read

Simon Spotlight
New York London Toronto Sydney New Delhi

SIMON SPOTLIGHT

An imprint of Simon & Schuster Children's Publishing Division

1230 Avenue of the Americas, New York, New York 10020

© 2014 Hit (MTK) Limited. Mike the Knight™ and logo and Be a Knight, Do It Right!™ are trademarks of Hit (MTK) Limited. Nickelodeon and all related titles and logos are trademarks of Viacom Intnernational, Inc. All rights reserved, incluing the right of reproduction in whole or in part in any form.

SIMON SPOTLIGHT, READY-TO-READ, and colophon are registered trademarks of Simon & Schuster, Inc.

For information about special discounts for bulk purchases, please contact Simon & Schuster Special Sales at 1-866-506-1949 or business@simonandschuster.com.

Manufactured in the United States of America 0714 LAK

10 9 8 7 6 5 4 3 2

ISBN 978-1-4814-0418-1 (pbk)

ISBN 978-1-4814-0419-8 (hc)

ISBN 978-1-4814-0420-4 (eBook)

Sparkie and Squirt were taking a nap.

Mike decided he wanted to do something knightly.

Their nap gave him an idea!

Mike woke up the dragons.
"I want to camp overnight
in the Tall Tree Woods!"
he said.

Mike hopped on Galahad.

He reached for his sword

and pulled out a cup of . . .

"Hot chocolate?" asked
Sparkie.

"I will not need that on my
campout," said Mike.

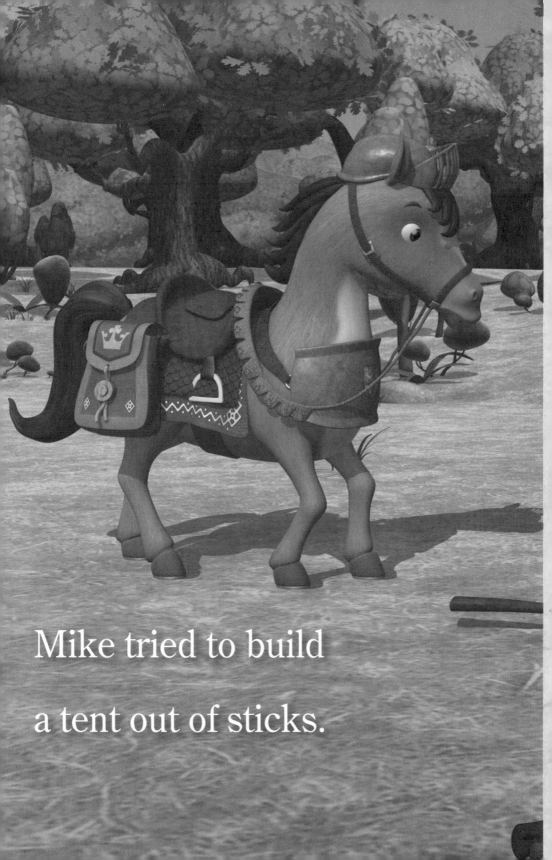

Mike tried to build

a tent out of sticks.

Squirt had a list of things
that Mike would need.
But Mike said he was going
to camp with nothing.
That was the knightly way!

But it fell down.

Finally, he got it to stay.

Then he saw that Sparkie and Squirt had a big tent to sleep in.

Mike gathered more sticks

to make a bed.

It was not comfy.

Squirt got out his bed.

It was very comfy!

"Do you want a blanket,

Mike?" asked Squirt.

"No, thank you," said Mike.

"I am camping out

the knightly way."

Mike bumped into his tent.

It came crashing down.

"I will stand on this lump."

But the lump was an anthill!

Mike ran around to get the

ants off.

"Here is a box to stand on!"

said Squirt.

"Here is a ladder!"

said Sparkie.

"No, thank you," said Mike.

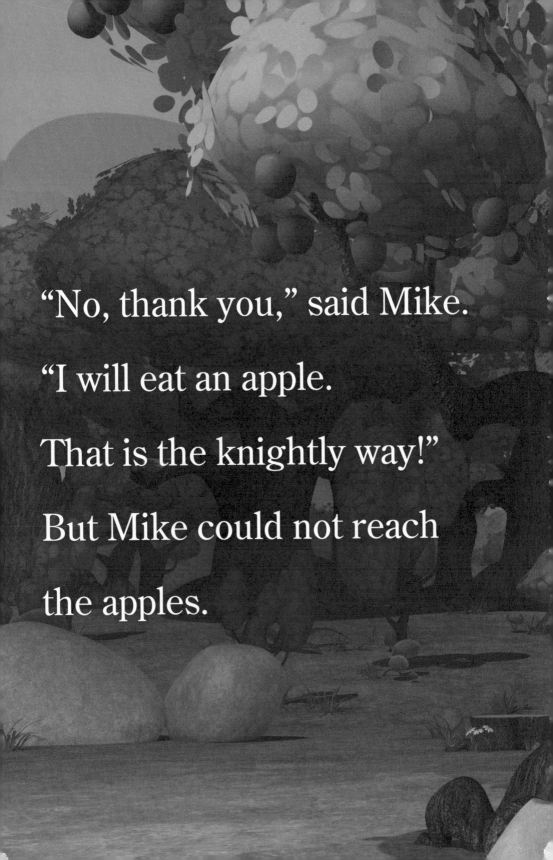

"No, thank you," said Mike.

"I will eat an apple.

That is the knightly way!"

But Mike could not reach

the apples.

Then the dragons made campout stew.

"Mike, we have some stew for you!" said Squirt.

"Oh no!" said Mike. "I wanted to do things the knightly way, with no help!"

"It is okay if we help,"

said Sparkie.

"As long as you sleep outside all night, you are still knightly!"

"I guess you are right," said Mike.

The dragons helped Mike fix his tent and gave him stew.

Mike shared his hot
chocolate.

Then they all went to bed.

They slept outside all night.

It was the perfect knightly

campout!